GREEK BEASTS AND HEROES

The Dolphin's Message

LUCY COATS
Illustrated by Anthony Lewis

Orion
Children's P

Text and illustrations first appeared in
Atticus the Storyteller's 100 Greek Myths
First published in Great Britain in 2002
by Orion Children's Books
This edition published in Great Britain in 2010
by Orion Children's Books
a division of the Orion Publishing Group Ltd
Orion House
5 Upper St Martin's Lane
London WC2H 9EA
An Hachette UK company

3 5 7 9 8 6 4 2

ISBN 978 1 4440 0068 9

Printed in China

www.orionbooks.co.uk
www.lucycoats.com

*For S.R. and H.C., wonderful friends
and the other two very intelligent members
of You Know What, with love.*

L. C.

For Anne and Vi

A. L.

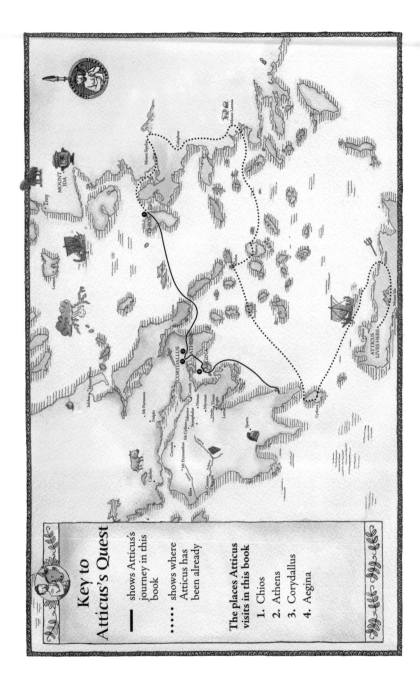

Key to
Atticus's Quest

— shows Atticus's
  journey in this
  book

····· shows where
  Atticus has
  been already

The places Atticus
visits in this book

1. Chios
2. Athens
3. Corydallus
4. Aegina

Contents

The Stories from the Heavens   9

The Starry Hunter   12

The Terrible Feast   20

The Dolphin's Message   28

The Bee of Wisdom   34

The Robber's Bed   42

The Sharp-Eyed King   51

The Runaway Sun   58

The Secret of Wine   67

Stories from the Heavens

Long ago, in ancient Greece, gods and goddesses, heroes and heroines lived together with fearful monsters and every kind of fabulous beast that ever flew, or walked or swam. But little by little, as people began to build more villages and towns and cities, the gods and monsters disappeared into the secret places of the world and the heavens, so that they could have some peace.

 9

Before they disappeared,
the gods and goddesses
gave the gift of storytelling
to men and women, so that
nobody would ever forget them. They
ordered that there should be a great
storytelling festival once every seven years
on the slopes of Mount Ida, near Troy,
and that tellers of tales should come
from all over Greece and from lands near
and far to take part. Every seven years a

 beautiful painted vase,
filled to the brim with gold,
magically appeared as a first
prize, and the winner was
honoured for the rest of his life by all the
people of Greece.

The paths through the mountains of Chios were steep and wooded and full of rustling noises. Melissa twitched her tail at the huge hunting dogs panting round her feet as their master talked to Atticus.

"Be careful if you walk across the island that way," he said, pointing to a mountain track. "I've seen a bear up there."

Atticus shivered. "Could you and your dogs come with us?" he asked. "I'll tell you a good tale as we walk."

The hunter clapped him on the shoulder with a huge hand. "Just make sure it's got wild beasts in it."

The Starry Hunter

Orion was strong and brawny, with muscles like tree roots, and a beard as black as midnight. He carried a club as big as a pillar, and his jewelled sword was sharper than knives.

His best friend and cousin was Artemis the huntress, and they used to run together through the woods and

fields with their pack of dogs, hunting anything which came their way.

Now the king of Chios was a cunning and crafty man. His island kingdom was overrun with wild beasts, and all his cattle and goats and sheep were being eaten up.

"If I call in Orion, and offer him my daughter in marriage, then perhaps he will rid my island of these wretched animals and I shan't have to pay him." He meant to trick Orion into giving him something for nothing.

 13

Orion soon agreed to the bargain, because he loved to hunt, and the princess of Chios was very pretty – but what he didn't know was that she was already promised to someone else.

For two weeks Orion hunted wolves and bears, lions and foxes, and at last there was not a wild beast left.

He brought all the skins to the palace and laid them at the king's feet.

"The marriage will take place tomorrow," said the crafty king. "But now you must get some rest."

As soon as Orion had fallen asleep, the king bound him tightly with ropes, and blinded him with a hot needle. Then he dragged him down to the harbour, and threw him into the sea.

But Poseidon the sea god was Orion's father, and he sent a great wave to carry

 14

him to the east, where Helios the sun god healed his eyes. Orion strode over the waves back to Chios, but the king had seen him coming and fled with his daughter to a secret place.

Orion soon went back to hunt with Artemis on the island of Crete, and she was very pleased to see him.

But Artemis' brother Apollo was jealous of his sister's friendship, so he sent a giant scorpion to attack Orion.

Orion didn't hear it coming up behind him as he ran with the hunt, and its huge sting flicked out and stung him in the heel.

When Artemis turned round and found her favourite cousin dead on the ground, she was furious with her brother. But she forgave him after he helped her to shape Orion's picture in the stars.

And he still hangs there in the winter heavens, his jewelled belt glittering next to his sword, the greatest hunter of them all – never to be forgotten till the world ends and the stars fall down from the sky.

The hunter had escorted Atticus and Melissa as far as the boat for the Greek mainland, but his dogs had made them both nervous, and even Melissa was glad to be afloat again.

Atticus sang a song to himself as the old lady beside him rummaged in a bag and offered him a dried fig:

"*Brekekekex koax koax*
Brekekekex koax koax
Feasting in our froggy lake
on reedroot stew and duckweed cake,
enchanting melodies we make.
koax koax

We croak of snails and mudflower mousse,
we croak of Tantalus, son of Zeus,
and how he served forbidden meat
and gave it to the gods to eat.
(His punishment did not taste sweet.)
Brekekekex koax koax."

Atticus thanked her. He was very hungry.
He'd been living on bread and olives for
much too long, and what he really fancied
was one of Trivia's feasts, with jars of good
Cretan wine. Perhaps if he told a story
about a feast he'd stop thinking about it.

"Do you know the story of Tantalus?"
he asked the old lady.

The old lady nodded. "I like a good
story," she said. "But speak up, I'm a bit deaf!"

The Terrible Feast

Once every month Zeus's son Tantalus went up to Olympus to feast with his father and the other gods.

"How magnificent!" he thought every time he went into the golden banqueting hall.

"How delicious!" he thought every time he tasted a new and amazing dish.

One day, Tantalus decided to have his own feast. "I shall invite all the gods, and it will be the best feast ever given on the earth," he said.

He sat down at a big table and began to plan. He ordered flowers and garlands, he ordered golden plates and cups set with precious stones. He ordered linen for the tables, and velvet cushions for the floor. He ordered dancing girls and flute-players and the best singers in Asia Minor to entertain his guests.

"But what shall I give them to eat?" he asked himself, scratching his head. "The main course must be something they have never eaten before, and it must be the most precious food in the whole world."

 21

Tantalus thought and thought, but nothing seemed good enough for the gods to eat. Then he had an idea. It was a terrible idea.

"My son Pelops is the most precious thing I have. If I kill him and cut him up and make him into a stew, then the gods will be honoured. And they certainly won't have eaten that before."

So Tantalus killed Pelops, and cut him up, and stewed him with herbs and wine in a cauldron.

 22

The gods
were all talking and laughing
and spitting olive stones at each other
when the trumpets blew to announce the
main dish.

"Smells good!" said Zeus, sniffing.
"What is it, Tantalus?"

But Tantalus wouldn't say. "Guess!"
he grinned.

23

Zeus took a bite. Athene took a bite. Apollo took a bite. All the gods took a bite. But after one chew, they spat their mouthfuls out onto their plates.

"Tantalus!" they all shouted angrily. "You shall be punished! You have made us eat your own son!"

And Zeus bound Tantalus in chains and whisked him down to the Underworld at once. He created a magical pool of water and threw Tantalus into it up to his neck. Then he ordered a magical tree to grow right over Tantalus's head, with ripe fruits dangling from it.

"The water will always be just out of reach of your lips, and the fruit out of reach of your hands," said Zeus. "You shall never eat or drink again till the end of time!"

Then Zeus went back to Tantalus's palace and brought Pelops back to life. All the bits of him were still in the cauldron or on the plates, except for one shoulder blade, which had been eaten by a dog.

Zeus gave Pelops an ivory shoulder blade instead, and all the other gods gave him wonderful gifts to make up for what had happened to him. The best present of all was a team of magic horses that ran like the wind.

Poor Pelops recovered quite well from his dreadful ordeal, and lived a long and happy life.

But Tantalus is still in the Underworld, and he hasn't eaten or drunk a single thing from that day to this.

Two days later, as they sailed past the island of Euboea, a boy yelled. "Dolphins!"

Atticus leaned over to look. Seven beautiful dolphins were leaping through the waves by the boat. They turned their heads and laughed then sped away again.

"Oh," said the boy, disappointed. "They've gone."

"That reminds me of a story," said Atticus.

The Dolphin's Message

Amphitrite lived in the underwater palace of her father, old King Nereus, together with her forty-nine beautiful sisters.

Each day they rode their pet dolphins among the coral and seaweed on the bottom of the ocean, picking up pearls and precious stones that had been polished by the waves till they shone.

Every evening they braided their long hair with the jewels they had found, and went to feast with their father in his great hall. Each had her own golden throne to sit on.

One night, after supper, King Nereus spoke to Amphitrite.

"My dear," he said. "As my eldest daughter, it is time you were getting married. I have promised you to Poseidon, the god of the sea, and I'm sure he'll make you very happy."

Now Amphitrite was rather frightened of Poseidon since she had seen him in a temper one day. He had struck his magic trident on a rock, and made a great storm come out of nowhere, and Amphitrite had been swept onto some sharp coral and hurt her arm dreadfully.

"Oh, Father!" she cried. "Please don't make me marry him!"

And she ran from the hall and leapt
on to her pet dolphin, whose name was
Delphinus. "Take me away and hide me!"
she whispered.

And Delphinus did.

When Poseidon heard that Amphitrite
didn't want to marry him, he was very
sad, because he truly loved her.

He looked for her everywhere to try to persuade her to change her mind, but it was no good. She was too well hidden.

Poseidon asked cross crabs and flickering fishes, he asked lumpy lobsters and odd octopi – he asked every creature in the sea if they had seen Amphitrite, but none of them had. So finally he went to find Delphinus.

"If you know where your mistress is, and you can persuade her to marry me, you shall have a place in the stars for ever," said Poseidon. "I really do love her, you know."

Delphinus could see that Poseidon was telling the truth, so he took the message to Amphitrite at once. She and Poseidon were married that day, and they went away on their honeymoon in a chariot pulled by seven dolphins.

As for Delphinus, Poseidon kept his promise, and if you look up at the sky on a clear night, you can still see him swimming among the stars.

It had been a long walk across to Athens from the coast, but Atticus and Melissa had reached the famous city at last! The wooded hillside smelt of the smoke of sacrifices as they stood staring upwards at the Acropolis, and the beautiful white buildings shone above them in the pale winter sunlight. An owl hooted in the trees.

"Athene's messenger," said Atticus. "Let's make an offering at her temple. This is Athene's city, you know. She won it from Poseidon in a competition."

The Bee of Wisdom

The great god Zeus was worried. He loved his Titan wife, Metis, because she was very clever and gave him good advice. But Mother Earth had told him that if Metis ever bore him a son, then Zeus would be overthrown.

Now Zeus liked being king of the gods, and he didn't want that to happen, so he challenged Metis to a game of shape-changing.

Metis agreed, and as she turned into a bee and buzzed about the room, he sniffed a great sniff with his right nostril, and sucked Metis up into his head.

34

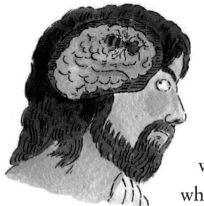

There she sat, giving him advice when he needed it, and tickling his brain with her tiny feet when he didn't.

It was rather uncomfortable, but Zeus just had to put up with it.

What Zeus didn't know was that Metis was pregnant when he turned her into a bee.

Soon Metis got very bored inside Zeus's head, and she decided to make some things for her new baby. She magicked herself a loom and some thread, and started to weave a beautiful robe.

Thumpety-thump, clickety-click went the loom, and soon Zeus had a headache.

 35

"Stop that!" he grumbled, but Metis carried on.

As soon as she had finished the robe, she magicked herself a little hammer and anvil, and started to make a wonderful silver helmet. Bashety-bash, crashety-crash went the hammer.

"Ouch!" roared Zeus, clutching his forehead.

Soon his headache was so bad that he called to his son Hephaestus the blacksmith to help him.

"Hum," said Hephaestus. "You've got something in there. The only thing to do is to cut it out."

So he took his sharpest chisel and split Zeus's head right open down the middle. Out sprang a beautiful goddess, wearing a shimmering silver robe and a winged silver helmet.

She kissed Zeus. "Sorry about the headache," she said. "I'm your daughter Athene."

As soon as Zeus had mended his head (with Metis the bee still safely inside), he invited all the gods to a feast to meet his newest daughter. He was very proud of her, and wanted to give her a present.

"I shall make her the goddess of wisdom and give her a city," he decided. "Perhaps that little one down there will do."

Zeus had just chosen the one place which Poseidon wanted to be his city. When Poseidon heard about Zeus's gift to Athene he was very angry. But there was nothing he could do to challenge his powerful brother's decision, so he decided to challenge Athene instead.

"Let us have a competition, dear niece," he said. "We shall both give the people of this place a gift, and they shall

decide which is the most useful to them. Whoever wins shall keep the city."

Athene agreed at once, and they both flew down to the city, landing on the flat rock the people called the Acropolis.

"My people of Poseidia!" cried Poseidon. "See what I give you!"

And he struck a rock with his trident. A stream of water gushed out and the people rushed forward to taste it.

"Ugh!" they said, spitting and coughing. "What horrible salty water! This is no good to us at all!"

"My people of Athens!" cried Athene. "See what I give you!"

And she pointed her finger at the ground. Up rose a beautiful tree, with silvery leaves and little hard round fruits. The fruits fell into a wooden barrel on the ground, and the people rushed to look in.

"Oh!" they cried in wonder as they scooped out oil and olives. "How useful! How delicious! Thank you, Athene."

Poseidon dived into the sea in a fury, and ever since then, the city of Athens has belonged to the goddess Athene.

The bustle of Athens was soon left behind as Atticus and Melissa walked north-west into the woods near Corydallus.

They stopped for the night at a tavern and when he had stabled Melissa, Atticus sat down and rubbed his tired feet while the man on the bench beside him stretched and yawned.

"Long day?" asked Atticus sympathetically.

The man nodded. "I'm exhausted. I only hope the beds are comfortable here – I could sleep for a week."

"Better not sleep too soundly," said Atticus. "You know the story about Procrustes? He had an inn round here somewhere."

The Robber's Bed

In the far-off days of his youth, King Aegeus had been secretly married to a beautiful princess of Troezen called Aethra. He had had to leave her behind when he went back to rule Athens, but he never forgot her.

"I shall leave my golden sword and sandals under this great boulder, my darling," he said as he kissed her goodbye.

"If we should have a son who is strong enough to get them out, then send him to me, and I shall make him my heir."

In due course, Aethra had a son called Theseus (the one who later killed the Cretan Minotaur).

When he was eighteen years old his mother called him to her. "That boulder in the garden is annoying me," she said. "Could you just move it for me?"

Theseus always obeyed his mother, so he put his back against the boulder and pushed. It didn't move. He pushed harder. The boulder moved a fraction. He pushed with all his strength. The boulder toppled over and rolled into the valley below with a crash.

Aethra stepped forward, picked up the golden sword and sandals and gave them to Theseus. "These belonged to your father, King Aegeus. Take them to him in Athens. He will know where they came from."

So Theseus packed a bag, kissed his mother and set off to Athens.

He had many adventures along the way, but the strangest of all happened near a place called Corydallus, just outside Athens.

As Theseus was walking along, he came to a deep wooded valley. It was dark and gloomy, and no birds sang in the

trees. The rain dripped from the leaves in
heavy drops and soon Theseus was
soaked. As night was falling fast, he
was very glad to come to a little hut in
a clearing with a long bench outside.

"Hey!" he called at the door. "Is
anyone there?"

At once a strange old man pranced
out. He had a great black beard, and huge
arms like treetrunks, but his legs were
spindly and thin, and he was completely
bald.

"Have you come to try my famous bed, young sir?" he said with a cackle.

Now this old man's name was Procrustes, and he was a very famous robber. He offered lonely travellers supper and the use of his bed for the night. Then he killed them and stole their gold.

Theseus was very tired, so he ate a good supper and then lay down to sleep. His feet dangled over the edge of the bed. Soon he was woken by Procrustes singing softly to himself:

"Chop the tall ones, make them fit,
Cut them up, then wait a bit.
Poke them to make sure they're dead,
Steal their gold, then make the bed!
Stretch the short ones till they're tall,
Tie them up then give a haul,
Wait till bones go crick and crack,
Put their gold in a great big sack!"

Theseus didn't like Procrustes' song one little bit. He had heard the stories about people disappearing around here, and now he knew why.

 47

He leaped out of bed and grabbed the old man.

"You will never kill another innocent traveller," he cried. And

snicker-snacker- snick

he chopped Procrustes into tiny little bits with the golden sword before he could sing another note.

When Theseus arrived at Athens, poor King Aegeus wept as he saw his old sword and sandals.

 48

"My son," he cried. "You are just in time to sail to Crete and save us from the dreadful Minotaur!"

So brave Theseus went straight off to Crete without ever getting to know his father properly, and of course by the time he returned, King Aegeus was dead. But that is another story for another time and another place.

Atticus and Melissa had waited for days before they could catch a boat from the mainland to the tiny island of Aegina. Now Atticus had lost his hat. He searched the ground near the harbour.

"Where did I drop it?" he muttered irritably. "I know it's round here somewhere."

Just then a little girl came panting along the path. "Sir, sir! You dropped your hat! I found it by the fishstall!"

"Thank you," said Atticus. "I'm fond of this hat – we've walked a long way together! Sit here beside me while I wait for a boat, and I'll tell you a story all about someone with sharp eyes just like you."

The Sharp-Eyed King

King Sisyphus Sharp-Eyes, they called him behind his back, because he never missed a thing.

If there was a missing coin, Sisyphus would be sure to find it. If a child hid his toy, Sisyphus would be sure to have noticed where it was hidden.

He was always stalking the streets of Corinth, watching what his people were doing, peering round corners and into windows until the people of Corinth were the best-behaved in Greece for fear that their king would catch them doing something they shouldn't.

 51

One day, as he was walking outside the city walls, he noticed a very pretty nymph disappear into a cave followed by a cloud of shining dust.

"Aha!" he said to himself. "That'll be Aegina running off with Zeus. I heard he was in love with her. Her father will be cross."

Sure enough, the next day, the river god Asopus dripped his way angrily into Sisyphus's throne room, trailing weed over the floor.

"Have you seen my daughter?" he asked. "She's disappeared."

 54

Sisyphus looked at Asopus and stroked his beard thoughtfully. "I might know where she is," he said. "What's it worth?"

After some hard bargaining, Asopus agreed to give Sisyphus a spring of clean water for his city, which was running dry after a drought.

"Now tell me where she is!" he growled, so Sisyphus did.

Asopus ran to the cave and burst in, roaring angrily and taking his daughter and Zeus quite by surprise. Zeus had left his thunderbolts at home, but quick as lightning he threw Aegina out of the cave door and right into the Bay of Athens.

"Become an island!" he yelled. Then he turned himself into a bit of the cave wall, so that Asopus couldn't find him.

 55

There was a great big splash as Aegina landed in the sea. Rocks grew out of her body, and earth covered her mouth and eyes, and she spread into a small island all covered with flowers.

It took Zeus a long time to find out who had betrayed him, but when he did, King Sisyphus Sharp-Eyes was made to feel very sorry indeed that he had ever interfered with the ruler of the universe.

A boat had come into Aegina's harbour at last, and it was one Atticus knew.

"Atticus the Storyteller!" bellowed Captain Nikos, as he and Melissa came aboard *The Star of the Sea*. "How've you been?" And he clapped Atticus on the shoulder. "Make yourself comfortable while we get under way, and then you can tell me a story."

As Atticus settled Melissa, he whispered in her ear. "I'll tell Nikos the story of Phaëthon. Nikos seems like a crazy driver too!"

The Runaway Sun

The Golden Gates of the East flew open, and out galloped Helios the sun god in his fiery chariot. His four

chestnut horses snorted sparks of flame from their red nostrils, and Helios had to hold the reins tightly to keep them on the small stony path through the early morning clouds.

Up, up, up the sky they raced, and as they got higher the earth below basked in the warm, bright golden rays that Helios wore as a crown on his head.

At the very top of the sky, the path started to curve down, and now the straining horses could see the cool Ocean of the West below.

Faster and faster they ran towards their open stables, and soon they were plunging and steaming in the waves while Helios's five daughters prepared golden bowls of hay and oats for them to eat. On earth, night spread her black cloak over all the lands.

Then Helios loaded his chariot and horses onto a golden cloud-boat shaped like a bowl, and set it sailing round the world, back to the Golden Gates of the East. There he slept in his sister Eos's palace until it was time to set out again.

Now Helios had an only son whose name was Phaëthon. He was a spoilt, whiny boy, but his father was very fond of

 60

him and one day he stupidly made a
promise to grant him anything he
wanted.

The very next morning, just as Helios
was about to drive off, Phaëthon came
running up to him.

"Father! I want to drive the chariot
today! I want to!!!" he wailed in his
whingy, mingy voice. "You promised me!"

 61

Helios knew he had to keep his
promise, even though Phaëthon's arms
were thin and weedy and not nearly
strong enough to control the great
chestnut horses. So he got out of the
chariot and handed over the reins. When

he put his dazzling crown on Phaëthon's
head, it was much too big and slipped
over Phaëthon's eyes, so that he couldn't
see very well.

Just then, Eos opened the gates, and
the horses ran through.

At first they stayed on the path, but
then they realised that their true master
was no longer in the chariot.

 63

They plunged down to earth, and the lovely green fields turned brown and burnt as the fiery chariot swept over them. Phaëthon screamed and hauled on the reins, and the horses bolted upwards to the highest heavens. Immediately the earth turned cold and dark, and a covering of ice began to form on its surface.

When Zeus looked down, he saw Phaëthon driving the chariot among the starry creatures of the sky and burning a wide path through the heavens. The swan stretched out her long neck and hissed angrily, the lion lashed his starry tail, and the bull put down his horns to charge. Quickly, Zeus seized a thunderbolt and threw it at Phaëthon. The chariot exploded in a blistering ball of fire, and Phaëthon was thrown out and fell to earth, where he landed in the river Po.

Helios ran to gather the broken pieces of chariot, and took them up to Hephaestus to be mended. His daughters rounded up the horses and took them back to their stables. But they were weeping so much at Phaëthon's death that the river Po became flooded, and several houses were swept away.

Zeus felt sorry for the sisters, so he turned their bodies into five tall poplar trees and their tears into drops of amber. If you go to the river Po today, you will still see poplars growing on its banks – and you can still hear their leaves whispering and crying in the breeze for the loss of their beloved brother Phaëthon.

"That was the best story yet!" cried Captain Nikos as they sailed southwards down the coast. "How about some wine, and then you can tell me another."

"I'll tell him about Dionysius," whispered Atticus to Melissa. "Dionysius invented wine, so Nikos should like that!"

The Secret of Wine

Semele was a mortal princess, with whom the great god Zeus fell in love. He married her secretly, hoping against hope that his jealous goddess wife, Hera, wouldn't find out. But of course she did.

Semele was six months pregnant with Zeus' baby when an old woman came to visit her, carrying a large basket.

"Rattles and toys!" she croaked. "Rattles and toys! Buy my pretty rattles and toys!"

Semele was delighted and bought several for when the new baby arrived.

"But where is your husband, my dear?" asked the old woman slyly.

 67

"My husband is the great god Zeus himself. He's too busy doing important things and ruling the world to be here all the time," said Semele proudly.

But the old woman didn't seem to believe her. "Does he glow in the dark? Have you ever seen his thunderbolts? How do you know?" she asked. "You should ask him to prove it, just in case he's lying!"

Then she went away and as soon as she was outside the palace, she turned back into Hera and flew up to Olympus.

Well, Semele lay awake all that night, wondering and wondering, and the next time Zeus came to visit, she begged and begged him to show her just one thunderbolt.

"Just to prove you really are Zeus," she said, fluttering her eyelashes.

Zeus took the smallest thunderbolt out from his bag, but it sizzled so scorchingly that it burnt poor Semele to death. Zeus only just had time to save the baby, which he sewed under the skin of his right thigh.

As soon as Dionysius was born, Zeus hid him away in a beautiful valley, where he grew up with the Maenads, wild dancing maidens who gave

 69

wonderful parties for all the nymphs and fauns and satyrs. All over the valley grew vines, covered in juicy purple grapes.

One day, Dionysius was bored, so he tipped a lot of grapes into a barrel and started to dance on them. The grapes squelched under his feet, and soon a lot of juice appeared. Dionysius scooped it into a cup, meaning to drink it, but the Maenads called him to a party, and he forgot all about it.

Two weeks later, a delicious smell wafted from the cup as Dionysius walked past. He ran over and drank it down, and that was how wine was invented.

Dionysius went all over the world teaching humans to make this wonderful drink, and everywhere he went, people worshipped him as a new god.

 70

Zeus was very proud of him, and even
Hera, when she had tried some wine,
admitted that it was as nice as ambrosia,
and even nicer than nectar. She and Zeus
threw a party for him on Olympus, and
there he was given his official title –
Dionysius, god of wine.

Greek Beasts and Heroes and where to find them ...

Athene's wisdom helped many heroes. Perseus discovered how handy it is to have a goddess on your side when Athene gave him something very useful to help him in his quest to kill Medusa. To find out what it was, read "The Snaked-haired Gorgon" in *The Magic Head*.

Athene was also famed for her skill at weaving. When Arachne boasts that her weaving is even better than Athene's, the goddess challenges her to a contest with unexpected results in "The Web Spinner". Look out for the story in *The Monster in the Maze*.

Do you want to read about Theseus's exciting voyage to Crete, the hideous monster he faced, and the real reason for his father's death? Then read *The Monster in the Maze* …

How will Zeus take his revenge on Sisyphus? And will the Ruler of the Gods be outsmarted again by the clever king? Find out in "The King Who Tricked Death" in *The Silver Chariot.*

Sisyphus had a very famous cunning son, and you can find out about one of his best tricks in the story called "The Greeks' Bargain." He also had a famous grandson. You can read about his amazing true dream of Athene (there she goes, helping another hero!), and all his adventures in "The Flying Horse". (It's in the *Greek Beasts and Heroes* book with that title.)

There are some more stories featuring jolly Dionysius for you to enjoy in *The Monster in the Maze*.

Greek Beasts and Heroes
the quest continues ···

The Silver Chariot

Atticus the Storyteller – and his donkey,
Melissa – set sail on a journey to the great
storytelling festival in Troy.

Wherever they go, people and places remind
Atticus of tales from times when gods and
goddesses and heroes and heroines lived with
fearful monsters and fabulous beasts …

Now it's *your* turn to meet:

Hermes – the messenger of the gods
Narcissus – who loved only himself
Pan – the god whose music was memory
The Fates – who weave the tapestry of life

Greek Beasts and Heroes
the quest continues ···

The Fire Breather

Atticus the Storyteller – and his donkey, Melissa – set sail on a journey to the great storytelling festival in Troy.

Wherever they go, people and places remind Atticus of tales from times when gods and goddesses and heroes and heroines lived with fearful monsters and fabulous beasts …

In this book are stories about Heracles, the bravest hero ever, whose amazing strength was tested many times.

How will he fare against a two-headed dog, a hideous giant, a horrible boar and a gigantic bull? Can he capture the prized, golden deer?

The rest of Heracles' labours can be found in *The Flying Horse*.

Greek Beasts and Heroes
have you read them all?

1. *The Beasts in the Jar*
2. *The Magic Head*
3. *The Monster in the Maze*
4. *The Dolphin's Message*

Available from May 2010:
5. *The Silver Chariot*
6. *The Fire Breather*
7. *The Flying Horse*
8. *The Harp of Death*

Available from August 2010:
9. *The Dragon's Teeth*
10. *The Hero's Spear*
11. *The One-Eyed Giant*
12. *The Sailor Snatchers*

 79